Scottish Terrier

Cross-breed

Ibizan Hound

Saluki
Chihuahua
Pug
Poodle

Bull Terrier
Chinese Crested
Bulldog
Dalmatian

First published 2009
by Macmillan Children's Books
a division of Macmillan Publishers Limited
20 New Wharf Road, London N1 9RR
Basingstoke and Oxford
Associated companies
throughout the world
www.panmacmillan.com
ISBN 978-0-230-71248-5
Printed in China

7 9 8 6

DOGS

Emily Gravett

Macmillan Children's Books

I love dogs.

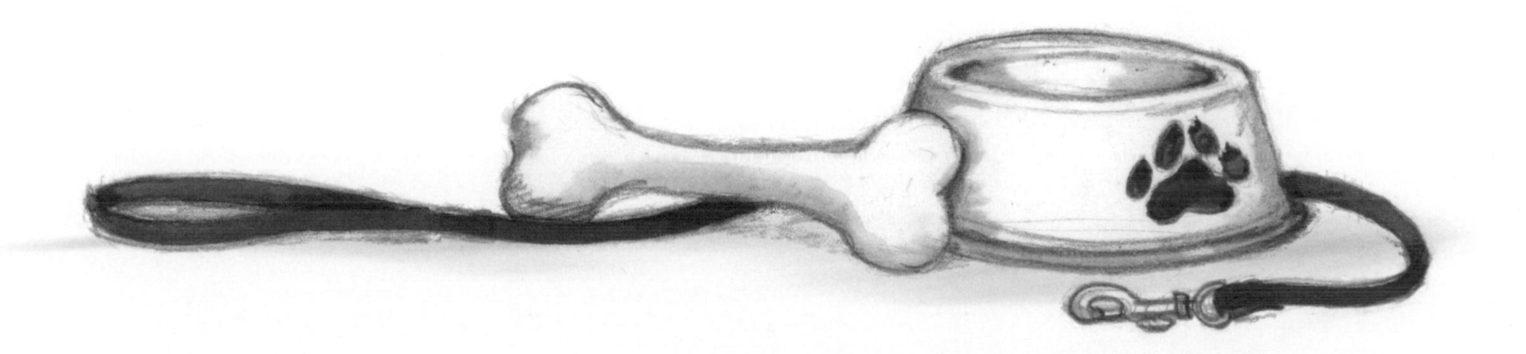

I love big dogs

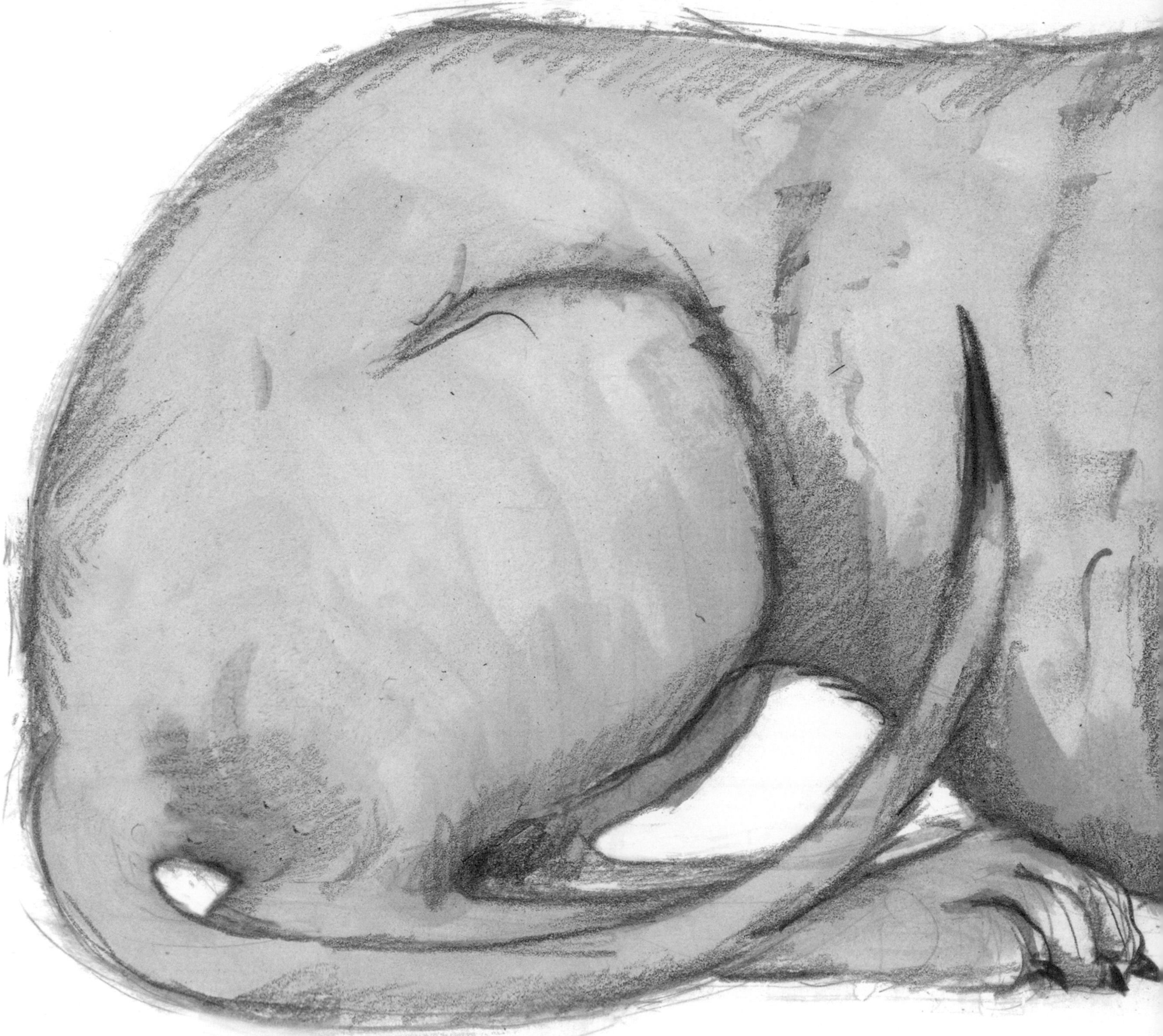

and small dogs.

I love stroppy dogs

and soppy dogs.

I love dogs that bark

and dogs that don't.

I love dogs that play

and dogs that won't.

I love hairy dogs

and bald dogs.

Stripy dogs

and spotty dogs.

I love slow dogs

and fast dogs.

Scruffy

and smart dogs.

I love dogs that are good

and dogs that are bad.

But the dog that I love best?
Let's see . . .

. . . is any dog

that won’t chase me!

Great Dane Dachshund Shar Pei

Bichon Frise
Airedale
German Shepherd
Jack Russell

If you liked DOGS, you'll love . . .

Keeshond

ISBN: 978-0-230-01583-8

Orange
Pear
Apple
Bear
Emily Gravett

ISBN: 978-1-4050-9022-3

Leonberger

"Gravett's expressive dogs are up there with Searle's cats and Thelwell's ponies"
Sunday Times

"Set to become a classic"
Independent on Sunday

UK £5.99
CDN $9.99

ISBN 978-0-230-71248-5